Splash!

First published in 2009
by Wayland

Text copyright © Claire Llewellyn
Illustration copyright © Lauren Beard

Wayland
338 Euston Road
London NW1 3BH

Wayland Australia
Level 17/207 Kent Street
Sydney, NSW 2000

Series Editor: Louise John
Editor: Katie Powell
Cover design: Paul Cherrill
Design: D.R.ink
Consultant: Shirley Bickler

A CIP catalogue record for this book is available from the British Library.

ISBN 9781526302281

Printed in China

Wayland is a division of Hachette Children's Books,
an Hachette UK Company

www.hachette.co.uk

Splash!

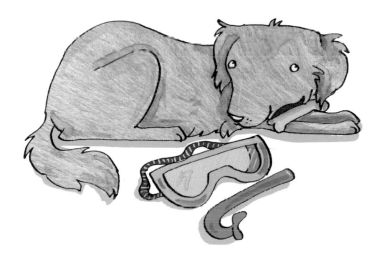

Written by Claire Llewellyn
Illustrated by Lauren Beard

WAYLAND

Where is my swimsuit?

5

Where is my hat?

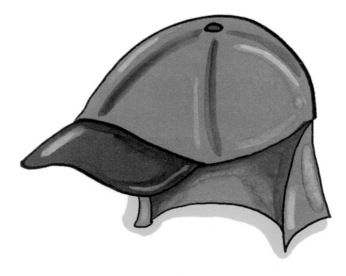

Here it is!

Where is my ring?

Where is my ball?

Here it is!

Where is my boat?

Here it is!

Where is my bucket?

Here it is!

Where is my mask?

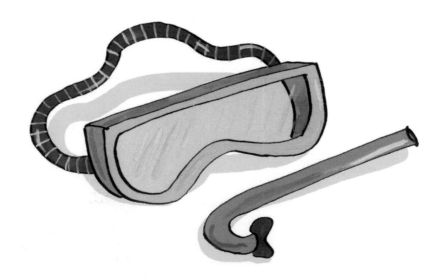

Here it is!

17

Where is the sea?

Here it is!

Guiding a First Read
Splash!

It is important to talk through the book with your child before they attempt to read it alone. This will build confidence and enable your child to tackle the first read without feeling overwhelmed. Look at the pictures together, read the book title, and pick out words of interest and the high frequency words for discussion.

The high frequency words in this title are:
is   it   my

1. Talking through the book

The children want to go swimming. They keep asking Mum where everything is.

> **Let's read the title: Splash!**
> **Why do you think it is called Splash?**
> **Turn to page 4. The girl is asking Mum,**
> **"Where is my swimsuit?"**
> **Look, Mum has it. She says, "Here it is."**
>
> **Now turn to page 6. What do you think the boy says on this page?**

Continue to read the book, with your child looking at the illustrations, for example page 20:

> **At last they're in the water. Splash!**

2. A first reading of the book

Ask your child to read the book independently and point carefully underneath each word (tracking), while thinking about the story.

Work with your child, prompting them and praising their careful tracking, attempts to correct themselves and their knowledge of letters and sounds:

Well done. You made it sound like a question. Did you spot the question mark?

Yes, 'water' makes sense, but this word starts with 's'. What else could it be?

3. Follow-up activities

- Select a high frequency word, as listed on p22, and ask your child to find it throughout the book. Discuss the shape of the letters and the letter sounds.

- To memorise the word, ask your child to write it in the air, then write it repeatedly on a whiteboard or on paper, leaving a space between each attempt.

- Alternate writing the new word starting with a capital letter, and then with a lower-case letter.

4. Encourage

- Rereading of the book many times.
- Drawing a picture based on the story.
- Writing a sentence using the practised word.

START READING is a series of highly enjoyable books for beginner readers. **The books have been carefully graded to match the Book Bands widely used in schools.** This enables readers to be sure they choose books that match their own reading ability.

Look out for the Band colour on the book in our Start Reading logo.

The Bands are:

Pink Band 1A and 1B

Red Band 2

Yellow Band 3

Blue Band 4

Green Band 5

Orange Band 6

Turquoise Band 7

Purple Band 8

Gold Band 9

START READING books can be read independently or shared with an adult. They promote the enjoyment of reading through satisfying stories supported by fun illustrations.

Claire Llewellyn has written many books for children. Some of them are about real things like animals and the Moon, others are storybooks. Claire has two children, but they are getting too big for stories like this one. She hopes you will enjoy reading her stories instead.

Lauren Beard was born in Bolton in 1984. She graduated from Loughborough University in 2006. That same year she came runner up in the Macmillan children's book prize. Since graduating she has had numerous books published and now works in a studio in Manchester.